IT'S ME, CHRISTY

original title: **Grandmother Orphan**

by Phyllis Green

cover by Gloria Kamen

SCHOLASTIC BOOK SERVICES

NEW YORK • TORONTO • LONDON • AUCKLAND • SYDNEY • TOKYO

Books by Phyllis Green available from Scholastic Book Services:

Nantucket Summer
It's Me, Christy

12 11 10 9 8 7 6 5 4 3 2 1   10   8 9/7 0 1 2 3/8

Printed in the U.S.A.   06

IT'S ME,
CHRISTY

For
Daddy, Sarah, Victor
and
Dick, Pat, Ricky, and Lynne

Contents

Sunday Night

My "Bad" Grandmother

Boy, there really were some oddballs on the bus. There were regular people too, of course. But the oddballs stood out.

Like Old Mrs. Crosslegs with her blue-striped dress and floppy hat and six shopping bags, always first off for the P-stops; the pimply college boy who stuttered and photographed every gas pump and telephone pole along the way; the toothless man who looked like Uncle Sam; and the eleven-year-old girl with the pixie haircut who had been expelled from school for shoplifting and sent to visit her bad grandmother.

That last oddball was me — Christy Clarey. I took something. The sixth-grade teacher found out and tattled to the principal, and I got expelled for a week. My dad and mother about had heart attacks, and after some fast phone calls presented me with a bus ticket to my bad grandmother in Teaneck, New Jersey.

We live in Pittsburgh, so it was one heck of a ride. I slept part of the way, and I cried part of the way. Who wants to spend a week expelled with a bad grandmother? I wanted to have fun and thumb my nose out the window to my friends who *had* to go to school. Who in Teaneck would care if I went to school or not?

I didn't even know this grandma. Grandmother Clarey, my good grandmother, lives twenty miles west of Pittsburgh and we see her often.

She is my white-haired grandmother who cooks turkey and apple pies when she knows you are coming to visit. She collects for the March of Dimes and plays bridge and has distant relatives who are charter members of the Women's Christian Temperance Union. She is about as round as a grandmother should be and she always wants to know how much I've grown, and would I please say *please* and *thank you* and *you're welcome* and all the other nice granddaughterly things. If she catches me saying a swear word she'll shake her head and sigh or else look the other way and pretend she doesn't hear it. She is really a good grandmother.

But Grandmother Matthew. Well, I didn't know anything about *her* except that she was bad. We never saw her. It was different when I was little, so they tell me. But she and my dad had a fight when I was five. I'm not sure he even remembers what it was about, but every time my mother mentions her name, my father grits his teeth. When I was expelled he said that if he had false teeth, he'd be working on his second pair.

Tony's not really my father. Nor is Sue Clarey my real mother. I'm adopted. I don't know who my mother is. Sometimes when I'm in a crowded place, like the grocery store, I think perhaps my mother is there. Is she the lady in the tight pink slacks who was nice to me and let me ahead in line? Or is she the one in green curlers and purple jumpsuit who snarled at me when I dropped the economy-sized mustard jar on her toe? Or does she live in Hong Kong? It's terrible not to know.

Before I stepped in her door that Sunday night, the only thing I remembered hearing about Grandmother Matthew was that she bleached her hair and was in her second marriage to a man named Mickey and they were both truck drivers.

The door opened. She looked tough and feisty. She had her hands on her hips and her mouth held a cigarette all by itself. When she spoke it jiggled and sort of stuck to her upper lip.

"So you're Christy, the little thief," she said. "Come on in. I'm your grandmother."

She put her arm around my back and led me to the hall closet.

"This is the closet," she said. "Your room is blue, at the top of the stairs. Don't fiddle in the bathroom. I'm having a cup of coffee. How do you like yours?"

How did I like mine? I wasn't allowed to drink coffee.

"Black," I said, hoping I wouldn't choke on my first cup.

She went to the kitchen. I whipped off my coat and hung it, not my usual way, but so that both shoulders were secure on the hanger and the top button buttoned. Then I raced my suitcase up the stairs, found the blue room and threw it on the bed. Then I ran back down the stairs and into the kitchen for *coffee*.

Grandmother was drinking hers and looking at a road map spread out on the kitchen table. My coffee was waiting for me. I sat down in front of it and stared at its blackness and steam.

"Mickey left this morning," Grandmother said. "He should be here now." She pointed on the map.

"Maybe I passed him on the bus," I said.

"I love the California run. It's my favorite," Grandmother said.

I don't think she said it to make me feel bad. It was more of a statement to the map. But I did know that if it hadn't been for me, she would be on that run with Mickey. They were driving partners.

I took my first gulp of coffee. Wow! It felt like it was eating away my gums. I swallowed it a drop at a time like medicine. It was horrible.

"I lied to you," I said to her. "I really don't drink my coffee black. I don't even —"

"The milk's in the fridge. Sugar's on the stove," she said, not letting me finish my confession.

So I doctored it up with milk and sugar till it tasted not too bad — sort of like sweet burned soup. At least I could drink it.

After our coffee, we moved to the living room. Grandmother turned on the color TV and started watching her programs. They weren't exactly the ones I'd have picked, but she didn't seem to care if I liked them or not, so I watched.

I kept waiting for her to grill me on the shoplifting thing. At every commercial I sort of tensed up. But Grandmother seemed to enjoy the commercials as much as the shows and never even glanced at me.

At ten o'clock the phone rang. Grandmother went to the phone in the kitchen. She had a special way of walking, as if she were propelled by her shoulders and bobbing elbows.

"Mary Matthew here," I heard her say. Then, "Oh, Mickey love, where are you? . . . Good. . . . Engine running smoother? . . . I miss you too, love. . . . Yes, she arrived. . . . Scrawny. . . . It's so good to hear your voice. What did you see today? Tell me all about it."

And then I guess Mickey was talking because I didn't hear anything for about five minutes.

Then, "I wish I could be with you, darlin'. Call me tomorrow night, love. Good-bye."

My bedtime at home is nine o'clock. Grandmother Clarey sends me at eight when I visit her. It was already past ten and I had had a long hard day on the bus. But Grandmother went back to watching TV without a word to me. After a few minutes, I opened my eyes as wide as I could and moaned.

"When do I *have* to go to bed around here?"

Grandmother looked at me as if I had asked to jump on a rocket to Mars.

"There's no timetable," she said. "You know where your bed is. When you feel like flopping, go flop in it."

What a challenge. I could stay up as long as I liked and I was as tired as a baby. I'd always wanted to see the other side of midnight. But it felt so awful getting there.

However, I decided to try. It wasn't too bad after the movie came on. It was rather exciting, and I got my second wind and was really enjoying a tense scene when Grandmother's words burst over the TV audio.

"So, you got into trouble?" she said and I knew she wanted an answer.

"Yes, I'm expelled from school for a week. I took some pantyhose at the drugstore when I was supposed to be at gym class."

"And your mother said you should spend the week with me."

"She said I wouldn't have any fun here." That wasn't exactly what mother said. She said I should be punished and punished good. And my father said the worst punishment he could think of would be to spend a week with Grandmother Matthew.

Grandmother laughed that Mother said

I wouldn't have fun and lit up another cigarette. It hung out the side of her mouth.

"Well," she said, "I knocked a lot of sense into your mother in her day and I'll knock it into you."

That was it. No "you naughty, naughty girl" or any of that "we mustn't take things that don't belong to us" kind of talk.

Grandmother went to bed at 2:30 A.M. and I stayed up for five more minutes before I flopped.

Two thirty-five. A record!

Monday

Shopping Day

Grandmother woke me up at six thirty. Before daybreak! I was dead, but it didn't bother her.

"Them's that don't know when to go to bed have a wee bit o' trouble waking up. Get dressed. Don't fiddle in the bathroom. We're going shopping today."

Wow! Shopping! I love it. Grandmother Matthew is great, I thought. What a way to cure a new shoplifter, with *shopping*.

We did go shopping Monday. For a new water heater. Grandmother's was on the bum.

14

There is probably no worse way to spend a day than visiting every plumbing-supply house from Teaneck to Hicksville on Long Island.

We went in a red Chevy pickup truck.

"Don't you have a car to drive around in?" I asked.

"Sure," Grandmother said. "We have six Eldorados parked in the garage in case we want to go someplace special. And what's wrong with this little pickup? It's the latest model."

I didn't say anything, but have you ever noticed how people look at you when you're riding in a truck? Like you're number one on the poverty list, or fatally diseased, or a farmer, or something?

Plumbing-and heating-supply houses are full of yellow toilets, pink bathtubs, marbled lavatories, furnaces, pumps, faucets, air conditioners, and other things of equal interest. The plumbers stand around reading catalogs, laughing with the salesmen, saying business is bad, and talking about elbows, fittings, and copper tubings. Grandmother had to talk with them all and hear a whole spiel on the water heaters.

I got so bored I closed the lid and sat down on a purple toilet on display.

We spent the whole day in the plumbing-supply houses, except for a hot-dog stop, and we ended up buying the water heater at Sears in Hackensack.

"Why?" I asked.

"Why?" she repeated. "Because plumbers are special people. I like to associate with them. I never met one who wouldn't make a nice father or brother. They're my kind of people. You should get to know some."

"But why did we buy the water heater at Sears?"

"It's a habit. I buy most everything at Sears. But I look around first in case I decide to change an old habit."

"Are we going home now?" I moaned.

"One more stop to see a friend of mine," she said.

She parked the pickup in front of the *jail.*

"What are we doing here?" I panicked. I had had to see the police over the panty-hose thing and I wasn't eager to see them soon again. They took my fingerprints and scared me bad with a serious talk. I just wanted to stay as far away from them as I could.

"What are you doing?" I screamed. Grandmother had gotten out of the truck and was opening the door for me to get out.

"I have to check on something I just thought of," she said.

"I'll wait," I said.

"You'll come," she said.

I slowly stepped down from the truck and followed Grandmother into the jail.

A blue suit with shiny buttons, badge, black shoes, and rough red hands walked toward us. It must have had a face, but I sure wasn't going to look to see.

"Well, Jack," Grandmother greeted the blue suit, "I thought you'd be on duty now."

"Hello, Mrs. Matthew. How are you?" the suit said in a friendly-enough voice.

"Look around, Jack," Grandmother said. "Is there anyone here you recognize?"

Silence. Very silent, quiet, still silence.

At last the suit said, "No, I don't believe so."

"Huh," Grandmother said, shrugging. "That's a relief. I guess she's not in the circulating mug shots yet. I was worried. I'd hate to have a nosy neighbor come tell me a relative of mine was hanging in the post office."

"Well, how is Mickey, Mrs. Matthew?" the suit asked, politely.

"Mickey's having a ball. He's on the California run this week. Tell me, Jack, do you still beat up the prisoners?"

The suit laughed as if embarrassed. "Why, Mrs. Matthew, where have you been hearing such things?" he asked.

"Do they still use brass knuckles or something that doesn't scar?"

"Mrs. Matthew, please!" he protested. "This kind of talk is embarrassing to a good officer."

"Well, tell me this, Jack. How often do you have to delouse the prisoners?"

"Now that does get to be a problem," he admitted.

My head began to itch.

"Could we see the premises, Jack?" Grandmother asked.

My back itched too.

"Sure, Mrs. Matthew. I'll give you the grand tour."

The suit took us through the jail.

"It's small," Grandmother observed. "I'm sure Pittsburgh has a really big jail. Would it have rats, Jack?"

"Well, I don't hardly know. I've never been to Pittsburgh."

"What's on the menu for today, Jack?"

"Well, as you see, we don't have any *visitors* today. But when we do, we usually send out for a hamburger and coffee."

"How about breakfast?"

"You ought to try a hamburger for breakfast someday. It's not bad."

"I suppose in Pittsburgh they have a kitchen where they can cook up some slop," Grandmother said.

"Could be," the suit said. "I wouldn't know about that."

We had finished the tour and were ready to leave. Grandmother turned toward the blue suit.

"Oh, Jack, what I really came to see you about. I wanted to check on the rule. I noticed when Mickey and I vacation in Ocean City, there is a sign posted that says all criminals must register before entering town. Is that the case here, Jack? Do we have to let you know about any criminals in town?"

I looked at the floor and shivered.

"Be sure to do that in Ocean City," he said. "But it's not a rule here. Of course we don't like criminals any more than they do."

"All right, Jack. Thank you. I just wanted to be sure I wouldn't be arrested for harboring a criminal. Good afternoon, now," she said. And we left.

I was so glad to get out of there and into that red Chevy pickup. When Grandmother started the motor and pulled away from the curb, I could have cried with relief.

After dinner, we hauled the water heater down to the cellar and Grandmother hooked it up. I wanted to watch TV. Some of my favorite programs are on Monday night. But she insisted I help her.

She must have put it together and taken it apart five times.

"Grandmother Clarey makes cookies and plays bridge," I said as sarcastically as I could.

She smiled, rather wickedly, I thought. "To each his own, dearie," she said.

"If you don't know how to do it, why don't you call up one of those plumber friends you think are so great," I pleaded.

"I would," she said, "if I didn't have the week off like I do. The truth is I'm glad to have the chance to tinker with it. I love plumbing. I think if I hadn't become a trucker, I'd have been a plumber. Of course, I have a lot to learn about it. But I love it. Hand me that funny doohickey wrench now."

She tinkered and I held the water heater and handed her wrenches and waited for us both to blow up right through the roof of the house.

At a quarter to ten, everything was connected once again and she said this time the job was done right.

We went upstairs.

At ten o'clock the phone rang. Grandmother went to answer it.

"Mary Matthew here," she said. "Mickey! How was your day, love? . . . You're doing fine. . . . Fine. . . . I'll let you talk to her. Christy!" she yelled at me. "Come talk to Mickey."

She held out the phone for me. I didn't know what to say.

"Hello?" I said. "Yes. . . . Eleven and a half. . . . Sixth grade. . . . It's okay. . . . About forty degrees. . . . No, we didn't have rain. . . . Okay. . . . Good-bye."

I handed the phone back to Grandmother. She seemed pleased that Mickey and I had got on.

"Well, that was our little girl," she said to him. "Yes. . . . Don't you worry about that. . . . We saw Jack and he scared the pants off you-know-who. . . . I miss you too, love. . . . Take care. Call me tomorrow night. . . . That's tomorrow. . . . Don't worry, I'm as strong as a horse. . . . Mickey, I say don't worry about me. . . . Good-bye, darling."

Grandmother turned to me. "Well, let's see what's on the TV," she said.

"Not me. I'm flopping." It must have taken me half a second to get to sleep.

Tuesday

At the Hospital

Grandmother woke me up at 6:30 A.M.

"Up and at 'em," she said cheerfully.

"Ooagguh," I moaned. "What exciting thing have you cooked up for today?"

"We're going to the hospital, so don't fiddle," she said.

"The hospital? Why?"

"Because when I found out I'd be home this week I made an appointment, that's why. Now let's get some speed in it."

I peeked out from under the covers. "What's the matter, Grandmother? Are you sick?"

She started down the stairs. "Huh? Me?"

she said. "I'm as strong as a horse. It's just a little checkup. I've been forgetting to eat my apple a day to keep the doctor away."

All the same I got chills in my stomach. Something was wrong. I felt it. I dressed quickly and went down to breakfast. Grandmother wasn't eating. And no coffee. She wasn't even smoking.

"Quit staring at me. I'm not supposed to eat before my tests. And I'd love a cigarette but I don't want them to see my lungs all filled with black smoke."

At the hospital, she left me sitting in the emergency-entrance waiting room.

"Wait!" I said before she disappeared down the long corridor with the nun. "How long will it take?"

She shrugged her shoulders. "It all depends. You have your lunch in that little sack." Then she was gone.

I rearranged my sitting position and adjusted for a long wait. It's a good thing. It was an all-day deal.

By ten thirty there had been one broken leg, one food poisoning, a heart attack, two broken collar bones, and I had eaten my lunch.

By eleven o'clock I had read through the March issue of *Popular Mechanics* twice. By eleven fifteen, I had read it backwards, which was more interesting.

At eleven thirty a screaming blond woman ran in with a small boy in her arms. After she had given her information to the nuns at the desk, she sat down beside me to wait.

The little boy sat on her lap. She said he was four years old. His lips were all puffed out to twice their size and they were red and blue and black.

"What happened?" I asked.

"I don't know why he did it. I've told him and told him," she said. "But he was playing on the floor with his little cars and saw the lamp was unplugged and he plugged it in with his teeth."

"Wow," I said.

The little boy started to cry. She cuddled him to her and rocked him back and forth.

"I don't know what I'm going to do," she said. "I'm separated from my husband and when he finds out — He thinks I'm incompetent anyhow."

"Well, just say it was an accident," I said.

"Hah. Not him. He'll never believe it."

"Why not? I believe it."

"Don't you understand? He's dying to get something on me."

Then she was called and went into a room along the long corridor. So many things were going on in those rooms. I felt lonely when she left. It was nice talking to her. I wanted to call out, "I'll help you. I'll convince him it was an accident." But instead I watched the big clock on the wall slowly, slowly move. And when she and the boy came out, she went right past me and through the door without saying anything.

Grandmother came into the waiting room. She had on sort of a white sheet tied with strings.

"How's it going? You can eat your lunch now."

"Okay," I said, not telling her I already had and was now starving to death. "What are they doing to you?"

"Don't ask. They're taking pictures like I was Miss World and making me drink gallons of liquid chalk and poking all over my gorgeous body. Well, I better get back. See you later."

"Okay." And she was gone again.

The hospital had a hospital smell. Well, I thought, if it makes me sick there's no better place to be. At 2 P.M. I was thinking how much fun I had had yesterday at the plumbing-supply houses. The pumps, the faucets, the purple toilet. . . . The nuns at the desk smiled at me. I weakly smiled back, wishing they'd say a little prayer that I'd get out of there fast.

After an hour's lull, things started to pick up. A body was wheeled in, all covered up. "D.O.A. Dead on arrival," the ambulance man said. "Girl, Caucasian, about seventeen, auto accident."

I wished I could get a look at her. I'm not really ghoulish. I've just always wondered why they're covered up. But they wheeled her into one of the rooms and closed the door. Actually I probably wouldn't want to know at all.

About fifteen minutes later a man with a

mustache and a woman in slacks rushed into the emergency entrance and went into that closed door. The girl's parents.

They weren't in there long — just enough time for both of their faces to turn chalk white and their eyes to be quite red. The woman sat down. The man began to pace, muttering angrily to himself.

"Shush yourself," the woman whispered, nodding her head toward the nuns.

"Oh, yeah," he said, "you thought it was fine for her to take the car whenever she wanted. Give her anything, that was your motto."

The woman found a handkerchief in her coat pocket and blew her nose. "She had a license," she said, defensively.

"So what does that prove?" he asked. "She was no Mario Andretti. She needed more practice."

"Go ahead! Blame me. Then you'll be happy," the woman shouted. "Don't you understand? Her life is over."

The nuns at the desk kept writing. I looked at the two of them screaming their hearts out at each other. I just had to do something.

"Please don't argue. You both love her," I said, softly.

The room became quiet. The nuns looked up and one of them frowned at me. The man cleared his throat but didn't say anything. He just looked like he'd be happy to kick me fifty yards. The woman looked at me as if I had interfered in something private. I felt awful.

Their doctor entered. They both went to him and he took them back to the room where their daughter lay.

When they came out, the woman was crying fresh tears and the man had his arm around her. I felt like crying too. I wanted to say, "I'm sorry. Your dead daughter is your business. I'm not normally a buttinsky, but I've been sitting here all day and I'm so bored and tired . . . and besides I'm adopted . . . and I take things."

I didn't say it. I just got up and moved to another seat and tried to get comfortable.

When Grandmother was done at the hospital, we still couldn't go home. We had to drive to her doctor's first.

Grandmother started the truck. "Well,

did you just sit on your fanny or did you learn something today?"

We drove out of the parking lot. I thought about her question. Finally, as she pulled up to the doctor's office, I had an answer.

"I learned that life is full of love and hate and sickness and death."

Grandmother pulled the brake, took out the keys, and turned to look at me. She seemed surprised.

"Well, aren't we being profound," she said.

I grinned. "I felt very profound and hungry."

Grandmother laughed. "This won't take long. Then we'll go home and eat."

I sat in the office with her while the doctor reviewed some of the tests.

". — so I want you to give up truck driving," he said, "and truck riding too. With the condition your kidneys are in, you don't need that bouncing around. And we're going to have to work on that blood pressure, too. I'll call you in a couple days when the results of the other tests come in."

Grandmother looked as if she were hypnotized. Long after we'd arrived home and eaten dinner she was still saying, "Give up truck driving? He's crazy."

I turned on the TV and nothing happened.

"I knew the picture tube was going," Grandmother said. "Well, that's that, then. I'm going to bed. I want to be alone and read a little."

"At seven thirty?" I shrieked. "What am I supposed to do? I sat all day in that stupid hospital waiting room and now the TV is busted and you're going to bed!"

Grandmother went up the stairs. "Like your mother said, this isn't exactly the amusement park."

I didn't know what to do. I walked around the living room one hundred twenty-nine times and then I went to bed.

At ten o'clock the phone rang. I was still awake. I heard Grandmother answer the phone. I don't think she had been sleeping either.

"Mary Matthew here . . . . Mickey, darling . . . . Where are you tonight? . . . Oh, Mickey, you're doing fine. I wish I could be with you. . . . I'm one hundred percent

A-okay. Yes, Mickey, I told you I was as strong as a horse. . . . Doc Gold says I'll live to be ninety-nine. . . . I'll still love you, then, too. Call me tomorrow night, love. . . . Good-bye."

Wednesday

Housecleaning

On Wednesday we housecleaned Grandmother's gray-and-white Dutch colonial. We started at the top and worked our way down through closets, mattresses, drawers, floors, corners, cupboards, curtains, windows, and rugs. We cleaned *everything*. Grandmother picked up speed as she went along while I got tireder and tireder until I just about collapsed.

"Isn't there a child-labor law in New Jersey?" I asked.

"Help me outside with this rug. We'll flip it over the clothesline and you can beat it," Grandmother said.

"Beat it? What did it do wrong?" I said.

Grandmother raised one eyebrow. "Are you lifting your share of the rug?" she asked.

"I bet you're the only person since 1900 to beat a rug. Hoover came out with a new invention, you know."

I ended up beating the dickens out of the rug. If you're ever mad, it's a great thing to do. Boy, could I swat it. I was covered with dust. Grandmother said I better stop before I polluted the whole neighborhood.

We had toast and hard-boiled eggs for lunch.

"Why are we working so hard?" I asked. "Why are we cleaning the *whole* house?"

"I always clean when I have problems," Grandmother said.

"What problems?"

"The doctor's report. Don't remind me."

"Grandmother," I asked, "why did you ever become a truck driver? Didn't you ever want to be something normal, like a secretary or a teacher or nurse?"

Grandmother lit up a cigarette and stretched out her legs.

"I guess it all started when Bobo walked out on me. He was my first husband. I told him to take out the garbage. He took it out and never came back. I had Susie, your mother, to look after. She was in second grade. So I got a job as lunch mother, serving in the cafeteria. One day the principal said he'd like to recommend me for a school bus driver. I said okay. And in a couple weeks, there I was, driving a school bus."

"Did he see you driving your car? Is that how he knew you were a good driver, Gram?"

"He didn't even know if I had a driver's license. It seems to me it went like this. One day he came into the cafeteria when I was storming and giving what-for to a bunch of boys. He said, 'You yell SHUT UP better than anybody we ever had working in this cafeteria. You'd make a great bus driver.' So I figured, why not? I applied for the job."

"Well, then, how did you graduate to trucks?"

Grandmother stood up and flattened her cigarette in the coffee cup.

"You don't fool me, missus. The more questions you can think up, the less work you think we'll do."

"No, honest, Gram, how did you?"

She began washing the lunch dishes. "Grab that scrub brush and start scrubbing and I'll tell you. I loved driving the school bus and that's the truth. I had those kids shaped up the first day. There was no screaming allowed on my bus unless I was doing it. I enjoyed the trip. I didn't have a car for taking rides in the country. I wished I could see more things. Oh, friends would take me but — Anyhow, about that time I met Mickey. Bobo had been gone about three years and I met Mickey and fell in love."

"Where did you meet him, Gram?" I said, as I scrubbed away the gunk under the stove.

"Well, I'll tell you this. It wasn't in the church choir. He was a truck driver and all he talked about was trucks and his runs and the sights he saw, and I tell you he gave me a powerful appetite for it. I thought I was going to bust if I couldn't see all those things too.

40

"He took me with him on a short run and I was hooked. 'Mickey,' I said, 'I'm going to drive a truck too.' 'Well, come on,' he said, 'we'll talk to the boss.' Well, we did. And that's how I became a truck driver. And you missed about five spots. Here, stand back here and you can see where."

"And you married Mickey and lived happily ever after."

"Yes, a few years later, when a judge declared that Bobo Buckhauser had deserted me. Yes, Mickey and I are as happy as you'll find anywhere."

I found the five spots. "My mother never talks about Bobo. Do you think she wonders about him sometimes?

I would if he was my father."

"She doesn't have to wonder. I could tell her where Bobo is. He's a bum, a drunk, a slob. Do you know where he is? He's a begging bum, right this minute. Maybe he's in skid row eating a chicken dinner at the Salvation Army or lying in a gutter in Chicago or in jail in Los Angeles. Any place a bum would be, you'll find Bobo Buckhauser. Thank goodness he isn't her real father."

"Who's real father?" I asked, confused.

"Your mother's. You know she's adopted just like you. You know about being adopted. What are you looking so dumb about?"

I was shaking. The sponge and brush fell from my hands to the floor. I stood up and my bones felt rigid. I thought they would break if I moved them.

"You're lying. She is not adopted. *I'm* the one who's adopted. You're mean and you're lying!" I ran over the wet floor and up the stairs to my room. I slammed the door and fell on the bed.

My mother? She never told me. All those awful things I'd said to her about wanting to see my real mother and never once did she say anything back to me. My head ached with the words.

"My own mother wouldn't make me wear these stupid leotards. Everyone else in sixth grade is starting to wear nylons 'cause all the junior-high kids do. You're just too cheap to buy me any. I bet my real mother would!"

I remembered my screaming it out to her. I think all my life I've been screaming "my real mother" at her. I covered my ears. I remembered the hurt on her face. I buried my head in the spread. The thing about being adopted is this: I've studied people. The only time they give something away is when they're tired of it or it's worn out or broken or damaged — so is that why they give away *babies*? I sobbed and sobbed till the bed shook. My mother was given away *too*? SHE NEVER TOLD ME! Or did she? In little ways — her shy little ways? But perhaps I, so worried about myself, didn't want to believe it.

Grandmother called up the stairs. "You've had enough time to wallow in your misery. Get down here now. We still have the cellar to do."

I decided then and there that Grandmother Matthew was the meanest creature on earth. She said she had to clean to forget about the hospital and the doctor's report. Well, that didn't mean she had to include me. I went down and I cleaned the cellar, but I didn't say one word to her. I just stared and wondered how any human being could be so mean. I was beginning to see what my father didn't see in her. She really

43

likes to run everybody. And so does my father, really. And maybe I do too.

At 10 P.M. that night the phone rang. I knew by then it would be Mickey. Grandmother answered the phone. They went through their lovey-dovey routine and then she asked where he was. She got all panicky and reached for the map when he told her.

"But you only made a hundred miles today," she said. "What's wrong, Mickey? You break down? . . . Yes . . . Yes . . . Oh, Mickey. . . . Mickey, you'll make up a little each day. . . . I hate carburetors. Now, please, Mickey, take it easy. You're all by yourself. Don't try for too many miles. . . . I'm going to be a wreck tomorrow worrying you'll be driving too hard. You got to promise you won't try to make it up in one day. You've got to rest. . . . Now, promise. . . . That makes me feel better. . . . All right, now, call me tomorrow night, love."

Thursday

The Other Side of Grandmother

I guess Grandmother didn't like my not talking to her. She got all nice and sugary with me on Thursday. She took me up to Bischoff's for ice cream at eleven o'clock in the morning and in the afternoon she made a big ceremony out of showing me her jewelry.

She really had lots. A couple jewelry boxes full. When I asked her how come she had so much, she said, "On a truck driver's salary you don't go to the poorhouse."

"But you don't seem like the jewelry type," I said.

She put her hands on her hips and shook

47

her head. "Honey," she said, "inside I'm just another Liz Taylor. I know I'm a truck driver. So I'm a gaudy truck driver. So kill me. I love genuine jewelry, Limburger cheese, old books, truck driving, jazz, plumbers, wrestling matches, Chinese food, winning arguments, and comfortable shoes."

It was good stuff, too. I had gotten a peek at some a couple times before when Gram had sent pieces to my mom. She was always mailing her jewelry to Mom with dumb little notes like "I don't have much time left and I want you to have these," or "My arthritis is killing me. I can't stand the weight of the rings on my fingers."

Mom would keep the jewelry in a safe place because she knew in a few weeks when Gram was out of her mood, she'd telephone and say, "I guess I was a little premature. Maybe you better mail my jewels back." Mom would just laugh and send them back.

"Go ahead. Try them on," Gram said. "They'll be yours someday. After your mother. See how they look."

"All right!" I said.

Gram didn't go in for little dinky rings. Everything was super sized. The soft yellow topaz she said was twenty-four carats. The aquamarine with diamonds on each side was twelve. The diamond she always wore was two and a half carats. She had amethyst, ruby, emerald, jade, turquoise, opal, and star-sapphire rings. She had a beautiful string of pearls. She had real gold bracelets and hanging diamond earrings. I put everything on and felt like a princess.

"Well, of course," Gram said, "it's not all to be worn at once."

"Of course," I said, but secretly I knew that when they were mine, wearing them all at once would be exactly what I would do. My friends would be so jealous they'd throw up.

"When you go home Sunday," Gram said, scratching her head, "maybe you better take these to Susie. That doctor's report and all. I don't know. It's not easy to be old."

I didn't say anything. I figured she could change her mind six times by Sunday.

We ate dinner at five o'clock so we could go to the early movie (a John Wayne, which Gram never missed) and be home in time for Mickey's phone call.

At exactly ten o'clock the phone rang.

"Mary Matthew here. . . . Mickey! . . . Now wait, now wait, tell me where you are. . . ." Gram studied the map. "Where'd you say? Mickey, you *promised*! . . . That's too long for any one person. . . . Something could have happened. . . . Well, it could have. Dang you, Mickey Matthew, what do I have to do to get you to stop that foolishness? Oh, Mickey, I love you so much. Don't do it. . . . Eighteen hours straight! You're killing yourself. . . . Now no more. Cross your heart and hope to die. . . . All right, good-bye."

Gram was a twitch. She started cussing and chewing her fingernails and chain smoking. We both sat in front of the broken television set.

"What do you want to do?" I asked.

We played Scrabble. Gram was good. I got g-u-t. Then she put m-i-g-r-a-i-n-e to it.

"What's that spell?" I asked.

"Migraine, a headache like your father gets. Does he still get them?"

"Oh, yeah, he does," I said, trying to figure out how to hook a *j*, *k*, or *z* on to the word.

"Tell him to lay off the chocolate. Completely lay off it. That'll be the end of the migraine," she said.

"Okay," I said. Ik? ek? ak? nj? ja? zi?

Is it too much to believe I lost the game? Gram was a real expert with all kinds of words like zisjch (an itch), yapke (a noisy dog), xip (a pimple), and schryl (a bossy landlord). We never had words like that on the sixth-grade spelling list. I couldn't find them in the dictionary either.

We went to bed at midnight. All in all, the previous days considered, Thursday wasn't half bad.

Friday

The Wedding Dress

Friday was even better.

"You know," Gram said, "I ran across something when we were cleaning the other day. It's an old box I sealed up thousands and thousands of years ago. I'm sort of curious as to how it looks. Do you want to see?"

"Sure. What's in it?"

"My wedding dress from when I married Bobo. Land knows why I've kept it around. I must be some kind of sentimental fool. Let's open the darn thing up."

She went to the attic and brought it down to her bedroom.

"Well, here go the years," she said, cutting through the tapes that sealed the big box.

She took off the lid. There were layers of tissue paper that crinkled as she opened it. She pulled out a long flowing dress.

"It *was* white," Gram said.

"It's beautiful!" I said.

Gram laughed, turning it around. "I'd never get into it today. Look at that waist, will you."

"I bet it would fit me," I said softly, while biting my bottom lip.

"Well, let's see," Gram said.

"Oh, Gram. Could I?"

She lifted it over my head and it sort of floated down around me. I was enchanted. I was beautiful. I was a *bride*.

"Try the shoes," Gram said, handing the white-laced, high-heeled slippers to me. They made me so *tall* and they were so hard to stand up on. I loved them!

"Now the veil," she said.

Then she looked at me and I thought I saw a tear come from the corner of her left eye and roll down her cheek.

"It won't be long," she said. "The years

go like a snap of the fingers. You're beautiful, Christy."

"Am I?" I asked. "Am I? Really, am I?"

She nodded. "Really."

"Oh, Gram." I hugged her.

"But don't forget," she warned, "the misery wearing this dress brought me. I only had one happy day. The day I wore it. It's not the dress. It's the man. Choose wisely."

"I will, Gram," I said.

"When I married Mickey I wore a simple light-blue silk shantung suit. But look what I got. Happiness."

"I'll remember, Gram."

"I was in a big hurry to marry Bobo. Don't ask me what the rush was."

"I wish I could go to a dance in this," I said, twirling around past the dresser and bed. My right shoe tripped over my left high heel and I turned my ankle. "Ouch."

"How would you like to go swimming today?" Gram asked.

I just about fainted. "Swimming? I'd love it."

"Let me make a phone call," she said.

"Wait, Gram," I said, feeling depressed and guilty. "I don't think my mom would want me to. She said I was to be punished. She didn't send me here to have fun."

Gram put both hands on her hips and tapped one shoe on the floor. "You're so young," she said. "I can't believe you're bad. I think you are the nicest little girl I've met in a long time and I'm going to take you swimming."

I went swimming at her friend's house. Lib and Doran Seeburg's. It wasn't a house. It was a mansion. Their indoor pool was the most fantastic thing I'd ever seen. It was completely surrounded by patio doors. I felt like we were outside. There were big green plants and ivy in pots and about fifty blue deck chairs and white iron lacy benches.

The maid let us in. The Seeburgs were vacationing in Antigua.

"Hello, Adelphia," Gram said. "Sure nice of you to let Christy swim this afternoon."

The maid smiled. Boy, did she have freckles. "Listen, Mary, Mrs. Seeburg tells me anytime you want to come here, you are welcome. It doesn't matter if they're home or not."

Adelphia had even found a pink bathing suit that sort of fit me. The bikini pants were just a little loose and everytime I jumped in the deep end I thought I was going to lose them before I hit the water.

"How did you ever meet these groovy people?" I asked Gram when I came out to rest under a sun lamp.

"Mickey and I play poker with Adelphia and her husband George. Lib and Doran watched us playing one night in the kitchen and asked if they could join the game. The six of us play every Saturday night that we're not otherwise busy. Lib and Doran are very decent people. They can't help it if they're rich. Poor Doran. Everything he touches turns to cold cash. He doesn't know why. The poor guy gets headaches trying to figure out how to get rid of it."

"Gee, what a problem," I mimicked. "Poor Doran."

"Don't laugh," Gram said. "It's not easy to be rich and not be a snob. Lib and Doran have done real well in the nice-person department."

"I'd like to get a chance to try," I said.

"So be as decent as Lib and Doran. They should get medals."

I jumped back into the pool.

"Gram," I called, "you don't have to watch me. You can go talk to Adelphia if you want. I'm a good swimmer."

"So I'll stay and watch anyhow," she said.

"Are you a lifeguard?" I asked.

"Look, smarty. I hate water and I can't swim a stroke. But one thing I can do is grab that long pole and fish you out if you get in trouble."

"I was only teasing," I said. I sure didn't want her mad at me. We were just getting to be friends.

She finally smiled.

I felt so tired but so great when we got home. Gram made a delicious spaghetti dinner with salad and garlic bread. I just ate and ate.

Gram wanted to read after dinner.

"What are you reading?" I asked.

"Right now? A mystery. I love mysteries. I bet I've read almost all of them. And I never throw them away. I'm saving them for something special. Hey, do you like to read?" she asked.

She found some old books that had belonged to my mother, and I got involved in a terrific Nancy Drew mystery.

At ten o'clock, the phone did not ring.

Friday Night

The Phone Call

At 10:01 P.M. Gram started to fidget. When she wasn't lighting a cigarette she was rubbing her hands together. I thought she would rub them raw by ten thirty. But that's when she started to pace back and forth from the living room to the kitchen. And while she was in the kitchen she'd stop for a minute and stare at the green phone on the wall as if psychically she could make it ring. I think she cussed at it too, under her breath.

"He'll call, Gram. You just have to be patient," I said.

She looked at the map and pointed to where Mickey had stayed last night.

"Something is wrong," she said to the state of Nevada. "I know it because I feel it here." She made a fist and pounded her chest, over her heart.

"Do you want to play cards?" I asked.

"It's something real bad," she said. Then she started pacing again.

At five minutes to midnight the phone rang. Gram stood there looking at it. She looked so scared. I wanted to hug her and say, "I'm here, Gram. I'm here with you."

After six rings she went to the phone and put it to her ear so calmly that I was proud of her.

"Mary Matthew here. . . . MICKEY!"

She screamed out his name.

I started clapping my hands and jumping up and down. She put her arm around my waist and pulled me to stand by her.

"It's *Mickey*, Christy darling. It's my Mickey on the phone."

"Mickey, why are you calling so late? I'm near a nervous wreck. I thought you'd call at ten. Christy and I have been beside ourselves. . . . Yeah, what? . . . WHAT?

Oh, no, Mickey. . . . oh, Mickey, no. . . no . . . oh, no. . . ."

Then she didn't say anything for a long time. She just listened and the tears rolled down her face and fell to the kitchen floor. I knew something bad had happened. She looked just awful.

Finally she handed the phone to me and she went and sat down at the kitchen table. She balled up the map and threw it across the room. She aimed for the sink but it missed.

"Hello, Mickey. This is Christy. . . . Oh, gosh. . . . That's too bad. . . . Are you all right? . . . Yes. . . . I'll tell her. Ed Funky. . . . Yes, I'll take care of her. . . . Good-bye."

I walked over to Gram and put my hand on her shoulder.

"Mickey's going to hitch a ride home with Ed Funky. He wanted me to tell you. I'm sorry he had that accident, falling asleep at the wheel. Will he really lose his job over it?"

Gram got up from the chair and ran through the living room. She threw open the front door and went out on the porch.

"Wake up, world!" she shouted to the sky

and the big Teaneck trees. "Mickey Matthew died tonight! Wake up, you lazy bums! I want to tell you what happened to Mickey."

I tried to pull her back in. "Gram, you got it all wrong. We were just talking to Mickey. The truck rolled over and it was demolished, but he was thrown free. He's okay."

"He's a dead man," she said, letting me lead her back in the house. I sat her down on the red sofa. "Truck driving is his life and now he's through. Falling asleep at the wheel. You just don't do that. He'll never drive another truck. He just won't. He might as well be dead. He is dead."

"Oh, Gram, there's a million things he can do instead," I said.

"I should have been with him. It wouldn't have happened then. I should have been with him."

I guess that's when I got hysterical. I started crying and bouncing all over the living room like a worn-out top.

"It's my fault," I wailed. "If it wasn't for me taking the pantyhose I wouldn't be here and you wouldn't have had to stay home with me and Mickey wouldn't have fallen asleep at the wheel and I want to die. I just want to die. It's all my fault."

"SHUT UP!" Gram said.

I stopped blubbering and looked at her. She looked like if I really wanted to die so badly she would be glad to kill me.

"Shut up," she said again. "Tonight, I'm having the breakdown. You can have yours in the morning."

I sat down and listened to her breakdown. She was sick for Mickey. He loved trucks so. Then on the other hand it was almost providential because the doctor wanted her to give up truck driving. But she couldn't give it up if Mickey was doing it. So now he wouldn't be doing it anymore. And now she didn't have to either. So it was good and bad and it all confused and tormented her.

"C'mon in the kitchen, Gram. I'll make you coffee," I said, helping her up.

She opened a kitchen cupboard and took out a bottle of whiskey.

"I don't want to start you thinking I indulge in bad habits," she said, "but tonight I need something a little stronger."

She sat down and drank her shot and I had a glass of milk.

"Well, we'll be leaving Teaneck," she said. "Mickey and I will just have to take up our retirement plans sooner than we thought. We had it all planned, you know. We wanted to open an old mystery bookstore on the Jersey seashore. All those books I saved and saved over the years are our starter. Now we can do it. As soon as he gets back, I guess. Unless Mickey has another idea. Matthew's Used Books. Doesn't sound too bad, does it? Or maybe it would be more friendly to say Mickey and Mary's Used Mystery Books. Yeah. I like that better. We both love the seashore. We'll get a place right on the boardwalk and live above the shop."

She put her glass in the sink.

"Tell Susie to send all her old mystery books to Mickey and Mary's on the boardwalk. Yeah. We won't make a fortune, but things will work out."

She looked at me. I yawned. It was 4 A.M. She smiled.

"Thanks, Christy, for hearing me out.

Tomorrow is your turn. We've sort of been playing footsie with your problem. We'll get down to brass tacks tomorrow. You'll talk and I'll listen."

We went to bed.

Saturday

Gram and I
Have a Talk

Saturday was my turn. By then we had
both calmed down. We slept till eleven and
Gram brought it up when she was boiling
her egg.

"What makes a darling girl like you do
what you did?" she asked.

She put two English muffins in front of
me.

"Well, you may not understand, but
everyone makes fun of socks and leotards.
I don't want to feel left out. I don't want
to be different. You're nothing if you don't
have nylons. All the junior-high kids wear

nylons. Mom said I was too young, but everyone's got nylons except me."

"I bet. *Everyone* probably means one big bum who leads her mother around by the string on her little finger. You're not in junior high yet. Pretty soon, babies in carriages will be wearing nylons."

"Well, I want to be like everyone else," I said.

"I can't believe that," Gram said. "You come from a long line of people who always took pride in doing their own thing. The only person I ever wanted to be like was me. Pour me another cup of coffee, will you, sweetheart?"

"Of course, the fact that you and I are even related is purely accidental," I said, feeling nasty. I thought she would be on my side.

"SIT DOWN!" she blasted.

"But I thought you wanted more coffee," I said.

She glared at me. "You're a mess," she said. "Every chance you get you put in some dig about being adopted. I'd like to thrash you."

I shrugged my shoulders. There was no

point in talking to her. What did she know?

She put down her fork on the red-and-white-checked tablecloth. Her head fell into her hands and I could hear the kitchen clock ticking. She got up from the table and came over to me and kissed me on the forehead.

"Was it really the nylons? Did they mean that much to you? I could give you boxfuls of them. But I think it's more than that. Is it just nylons that's breaking your heart?"

I started to cry.

"Well, I do want some," I sniffed. "But I don't know why I took them. I feel terrible when I think about it. I just wish. . . . Well, it's about my real folks. I mean, *what's wrong with me*? Why did they give me up?"

I had said it. The terrible words. *What's wrong with me?*

Gram sat down and tapped her finger on the table. She looked up at the ceiling and down at the floor. Finally she spoke.

"They gave you up because they knew you needed love and at the time circumstances were such that they could not give it to you. The most loving thing they could do was give you up so Sue and Tony could love you. Believe me, they think about you, too, *often*, and hope they did the right thing and that you are feeling fine and happy. Christy, *there's nothing wrong with you.* You just have the old "adopted blues." Your mother had the same thing, only with her it showed up as hypochondria. She always had a cold or a headache or a sore throat — anything to get attention. I don't know if I cured her too well because apparently she never told you she was adopted. Maybe *she'd* better come and spend a week with me. She could have set you straight herself if she had told you. Then again, I guess we all have secrets we don't like to talk about."

"No. She never told me," I whispered. "At least I don't think she did."

"Well, she had a bad case. And she was always shy and kept things to herself. But you, my little extrovert, you're so much like me I think perhaps you are me, reborn. Now just tell me in plain language: What's wrong with being adopted?"

"Oh, Gram," I said, "that's a dumb question. I thought you were above that. I suppose you'll make me finish my English muffin because children are starving in China."

"So maybe you're talking to somebody who knows more about it than you do."

"Are you an expert on being adopted?" I asked. She got a funny look on her face. She stood up and took the dishes over to the sink as if she were nervous. Even her voice shook.

"No," she said, "on the contrary. I'm the expert on *not* being adopted. If your mother didn't tell you about herself, she surely didn't breathe a word about me. I sure don't know one thing about being adopted. But I know what it feels like to be passed by time and time again. I know what it's like to live in an orphanage for eighteen years. I know what it is to hope the next set of parents to come through the door will say 'You!' and I know what it is when they don't say it. You get a peculiar green ache right here in the stomach. Others say it's in the heart. But my ache was always in the stomach. I had the kind of face nobody exactly fell in love with when they looked at it. Kids came and went. Kids got picked to be adopted. But I always remained.

"No, I can honest to gosh say I don't know what it feels like to be adopted. I guess that's why I'm such a fool about adopted babies. I guess that's why I adopted your mother."

She was at the kitchen window now, staring out at the rain.

"It's spring at last," she said.

I cleared my throat. My head felt empty. I was adopted. My mother was adopted. My grandmother was an orphan. Grandmother Orphan? What a weird family. Maybe this was what you call a heritage. From generation to generation we adopt ourselves? Grandmother Matthew an orphan? No.

"I don't believe you," I said. "You're making it up."

She turned to me. She smiled. "I was a foundling left on the doorstep of the orphanage, only hours old. Somehow I survived to spend the first year of my life flat on my back. The orphanage was filled to overflowing. There was no one to pick me up to feed me, or help me to stand or sit.

I was one of many and they tell me I didn't try to help myself. Maybe I sensed I had a dim eighteen years ahead of me. Mary Doe, I was, for five years. Then someone got the idea to call me Mary Smith. As I got older I worked hard at the orphanage. I scrubbed floors and took care of the little ones who got snapped up so fast for adoption. Each one that went broke my heart. Not because they were going, but because I wasn't.

"We had one nice director of the orphanage for a while. A Miss Snavely. She was a great help to those of us who were never chosen. She helped to make life bearable. But then we had a Mrs. Jenkins who spent all her time giving us lectures on cleanliness and godliness and morals and manners. And we had a Miss Love who didn't know what the word meant. So when I was eighteen years old I could go out on my own in the world. I worked a few months, then I met Bobo and married him in a week. And you know how that turned out."

I didn't like the tear that sneaked out of my eye and rolled down along my nose. I didn't want to feel sorry for her. What about me? I wanted her to feel sorry for

me. But she thought I was so lucky to be
adopted. And I guess I was. Mother and
Dad were darling. Poor Gram. She never
had a mother, never, ever. Never had a
mother! I watched her wash the dishes. She
looked sad, as if she were back in the orphanage wishing for someone to pick her.

*We want you to be our little girl, Mary.
We pick you!* I looked at her face. She was
probably never pretty. I supposed most people would look for prettiness first in a child.
Well, they don't know what they missed
when they didn't pick Gram. They missed
the best kid of all.

I wished I could have been there. I'd
have picked her. *I'd* have seen her smile
with happiness. I'd have been her mother.

Was it too late?

I ran over to the sink and hugged her.
"Oh, Gram!" I said. "I have a great idea!
I want to adopt you as my child because I
want you to know how nice it is to have a
mother!"

Gram kept doing the dishes.

"Gram, don't you hear me?" I said. "I
pick *you*."

She dried her hands. Then she put them

on my shoulders and we stood face to face.

"It's a little late for me, Christy, but I appreciate the thought. When you're grown up and married, I hope you have babies of your own, but I hope you'll also consider adopting a little child yearning for love."

We both burst out crying.

"Oh, Gram," I said.

"Oh, Christy," she said.

We cried all over the dishes and had to wash them again.

When we finished, Gram said, "Let's call Pittsburgh."

So we talked to Mom and Dad and I apologized and said I'd see them tomorrow night, and honestly I was anxious to see them again, to throw my arms around them.

Then Gram made me go up to my room because she said she wanted to have a private talk with my mom and I wasn't to hear.

Later, Gram went uptown and she made me stay home by myself. When she came back she had a package that she acted very mysterious about.

That night Mickey phoned on his way

home with Ed Funky. He said he'd be in Teaneck in two or three days. Gram told him about the color TV not working and he said they'd better pick out a new set when he got back.

Gram and I felt real comfortable with each other that night. We had had quite a week.

"I'm going to miss you, Gram," I said. "I could almost stay with you forever."

"Don't be silly," she said. "I'm like New York City. A nice place to visit, but you wouldn't want to live here. Come visit me often, dear."

"We should!" I said. "I don't know why my dad doesn't like you."

She shrugged. "I'm a little hard to take sometimes. But if you can get them to come and see me, I'll try to be on my good behavior. Sometimes I'm just a bossy old fool."

"Tell me some more about the orphanage," I said.

"Now let's get this straight," she said, "my early years weren't all that bad. Let me tell you about the time we put the caterpillar in Mrs. Jenkins' sheets. Well, there was such screaming as you never heard in your life. And have you ever had pie in your face or felt the thrill of throwing one? Well, we had this fair one spring and . . ."

Gram had me giggling all evening with her crazy experiences at the orphanage. She still talked with a cigarette hanging out of her mouth and she still didn't look like a grandmother. But now I knew what she was like inside. I knew all her toughness was so no one could guess how lonely she had been as a girl — the hard times she had gone through bringing up my mom alone, and maybe the loneliness in the fact that she hadn't borne a baby of her own. I wondered about that. I wanted to ask her. But I didn't. I would give her privacy on that.

But my mom and dad. Sue and Tony. They *were* MY MOM AND DAD. So why didn't they have other kids? Maybe they just needed to know I wouldn't be jealous of a natural-born brother or sister. I would somehow have to let them know it would be a neat idea. Of course I wouldn't bug them about it. I would let it be up to them. I guess I don't have to run everything.

And them. THEM. My biological mother and father. The great unknown. How did I feel about them now? Would I still look for them in the grocery store and in the movie line? I suppose I'll always be curious. I can't help that. But maybe I can make it a small part of my life instead of the big thing it's been. Maybe some day I won't even think about it.

Sunday

Going Home

Well, the mysterious package was for me, but Gram said I couldn't open it till I got on the bus.

I sat down in an empty two-seater near the middle and tore the paper off. Oh, that Gram. It was six pairs of nylon pantyhose with a note: "Your mom gave me permission to buy these for you. But they are not to be worn till your first day in junior high. Love, Gram."

Six pairs! I put them in my tote bag. That was nice, I thought, but not even necessary. Now I wasn't sure I wanted to be like every other kid. I even liked being different. I *felt* like a different person. I didn't even laugh when I saw one of the oddballs from last Sunday's ride get on the bus. It was the toothless old man who looked like Uncle Sam. I didn't even groan when he sat down in the seat beside mine and I discovered his breath was bad.

"Well," he said, "how was your week?"

Gee, he remembered me too. All those people on the bus and he noticed *me*.

"Okay," I said. "How was yours?"

"If I never should see my cousins again it will be too soon. Want to play a little cards?" he asked, getting a deck out of his pocket and resting his suitcase on his right knee and my left.

I looked at his white goatee and his toothless puckered-up mouth. He seemed real nice. It would be fun playing cards with him.

"Shall we play Fish or Slap Jack?" I asked.

He winced. "You don't know poker?"

I shook my head.

"So, let's do Slap Jack," he said, resigned.

Yeah, he was nice. I mean really. Not an oddball. A person — like me.